# Demetra's curse

# By

# Tiffany Blanton

Case ID: 1-13291989249

Paperback ISBN: 978-1-304-77478-1

Hardcover ISBN: 978-1-304-79686-8

# Table of Contents

# Chapter 1
# Dreams

She watched the edge of the sword slice through the flesh of her arm, as the blood dripped from the sword Demetra covered the wound with her hand. Instantly Demetra knew she was in trouble and needed to find a place to hide and quick! Suddenly all of the adrenaline that she had surged through her body, leaping up she kicked the sword from the creatures hand and jumped into the air as if she had rockets under her boots. Grabbing the sword she punched it through his chest. She stared deep into his coal black eyes as the creature's body fell and he took his last breath. Demetra fell to her knees and the pain from her wound surged down her arm. Not only did her wound pain her, but she was out of breath and was terribly tired. She located a huge hole at the bottom of a great maple and crawled her way there quietly and unnoticed. Demetra ripped a piece of her bloodied sleeve and used it as a bandage to wrap her wound. As she sat against the inside of the tree to catch her breath, she could not help but wonder if humans really deserved to live the lives that they were blessed with. She could just imagine them going about their everyday lives with no worries, no cares; taking every breath that she was fighting for, for granted. Unaware that there is a world that exists so closely to them that was fighting to keep them safe; allowing them to continue to live out their foolish ways. Was there truly a greater purpose she thought? Suddenly, the Earth began to shake violently! The roots of the maple began to break the Earth's surface. All of a sudden, Demetra dropped from the bottom of the tree. She let out a blood curdling scream…and woke up with a gasp! Trying to catch her breath, she found herself in her own bed! She grabbed her arm reassuring herself that it was fine. She wiped the beads of sweat from her forehead, and scrambled out of bed to open the window. She sucked the cool, fresh air deep into her lungs, and tried to calm her racing heartbeat. Another dream! She simply *could not* believe it! She *really* needed to stop reading so late into the night. Outside Rooty was crowing, loudly, assuring everyone that the day was about to begin. After yelling at him for being so loud she shut the window. She gathered her clothes and headed to the bathroom. She pulled a light yellow wash cloth down from the shelf and lathered it with soap and water. After washing her face she wrestled to put her long curly brown hair into a ponytail and tied it with a blue ribbon. "Demetra Scott!" her mother shouted from downstairs. "You need to hurry up! Your breakfast is getting cold!" She quickly got dressed and headed downstairs to grab some breakfast with her parents. When she sat down at the breakfast table, her father reminded her that Charlie's birthday was next Tuesday. "Thank you for reminding me, I had almost forgotten. But these dreams I've been having, have been driving me nuts! I had *another* one last night! This time the dream was *slightly* different," she said. "I was in the middle of a battle. There I was, face to face with a huge beastly creature littered with battle scars. Its chest was protected with a black leather breastplate. Mom, I could actually smell its stinking, fowl breath as our swords clashed. The creature had sharp, jagged teeth with particles of food stuck in them, which were obviously remnants of its last meal. Its face was hideous, and he had a large scar that stretched across his right eye which made it a milky white color. His body was covered in ash and his one eye was a jet black color, it was as dark as the other eye was light. He sliced my arm open with the blade of his sword. And just as I jumped into a hole in a tree to hide, the bottom of the tree fell out from under me and I just kept falling and falling! It felt like I was *really* there this time mom! I could *feel* the pain in my arm when I woke up!" Her mother laughed it off and told her that she needed to keep her head out of

6

those crazy books. Her mother told her she should really concentrate more on her schoolwork. That was *exactly* what she had expected her mother to say! The truth was that Demetra loved books. Books that took her mind far away to unknown and mysterious places. She loved books that were filled with adventure, mystery, and fantasy. Books that allowed her imagination to soar, to fly…far, far away. Demetra could just not understand why her mother never understood, that reading about all those places and things made her happy. Growing up in a small town like Wickets Hollow, where nothing much ever happened, just made her want to read more. The people here mainly tended to their families and their farms. The only other thing that Demetra enjoyed, as much as she enjoyed reading, was farming. She loved farming just as much as she loved her books. She had always been fascinated with the way things grew. Thank goodness her father was a farmer. Demetra would like nothing better than to lie beside his wheat or corn rows, daily…for hours, but she did have to go to school. Even during the school term, she assisted her father on the farm as much as possible. She loved being able to watch the seeds sprout from the earth and proudly present themselves to the world. Demetra had always felt a strong pull to the earth. There was nothing more she would rather do than kick off her shoes and dig her toes into the soil. Somehow, it calmed her. If she had a bad day, or if something was bothering her, she could always dig her toes into the dirt and a solution for her problems would just come to her. Being a farmer's daughter there was NEVER enough money to do anything special. But on special occasions, like Charlie's birthday, her mother always tried to make a special treat for dessert. The red apples seen in the sink, were a dead giveaway that momma's award-winning apple pie; would be waiting to meet Charlie and I at the door after school. Demetra looked up at the clock, gobbled up the rest of her eggs, washed them down with fresh milk her father just brought in, and rushed out the door. At the end of the lane, she met her best friend, Charlie O'Connor. They had been best friends since they were babies and this year, they were lucky enough to be placed in the same class together. You could see Charlie coming from a mile away. Charlie was tall, and his smile reached you way before he did. He was only fourteen, but he looked like he was twenty. Charlie's father, John O'Connor, and Demetras' father were close friends also. They were always there to help each other when one or the other needed it. Charlie's mother passed unexpectedly from pneumonia, two years back. So, momma took Charlie and Mr. O'Connor under her wing. She always seen to it that Charlie and his father had food in there bellies, a warm bed to sleep in and she even patched the holes; Charlie and his father managed to put in their britches daily. Even though Charlie had been through such a challenging time, with his mother's passing, not to mention that he and his father were not in any better financial shape than our family, he always kept a smile on his face *even* when things were not so great. He always had a way of making things seem so bright. I have to say I had always admired Charlie. On the way to school she could not help noticing that the air was very cold, which was rather unusual, for this time in March. "Dang Charlie, spring can spring any time it's ready!" Demetra exclaimed. The fog was so thick they could hardly see their hands in front of their faces. It was a silvery gray, and so heavy with moisture that it collected on their faces and clothes. Demetra couldn't help wishing that she had worn an extra shirt to help block out the cold that was shivering down her spine. "I wonder what Mr. Kirk has in store for us today," Charlie asked. "There is no telling Charlie," Demetra replied. They arrived at school just in time to take their seats before the bell rang. Demetra noticed that Mr. Kirk was not at his desk as he usually was. He was *never* late! As a matter of fact, Demetra could not ever remember a day that Mr. Kirk was not sitting in his chair when they arrived, his foot tapping impatiently, waiting for them. Mr.

Kirk was their teacher, and he was always watching her and Charlie. Just like they were a plague that was about to spread and kill the entire human race! She would catch glimpses of him peering over his glasses, looking at them, studying them…just like they were germs under his microscope. He watched them during lunch, and while they were at break. He was *constantly* watching them! He acted so sneaky and mysterious, all the time, as if he was hiding something, as if he knew something; that they didn't. He even made her and Charlie sit in the *very front row* in class. Demetra just could not figure out why, it was like she was always in trouble, but it was *exactly* the opposite. She was **never** in trouble; she made good grades and minded her own business, as did Charlie. She always wondered what Mr. Kirk was up to; he made her feel really creepy. You'd have to describe Mr. Kirk as a funny, prissy, little man always dressed in a starched and pressed suit, with a crisp bow tie and horn rimmed glasses…kind of nerdy looking, but boy; was he smart. He was so smart he could answer just about any question you asked but; he really was weird sometimes. Just as the bell rang the door flew open as if a tornado had just blown into the classroom and in walked Mr. Kirk. He walked briskly to his desk, and as he put his leather satchel down, he said, "Today class I have a big announcement! Next Tuesday we will be taking a class field trip to Stonehenge which is on nearby Salisbury Plain. I will pass out permission slips to each of you that must be signed and returned to me by this Friday or you will be ineligible to participate. Class, it might be a good idea to wear tennis shoes due to the terrain being a little rocky," Mr. Kirk explained. He also explained that since it was such a long ride students might want to wear pants and a jacket to keep warm. Mr. Kirk took a slight turn toward the chalk board allowing a ray of sunshine to glimmer off the buckle of his satchel. When it did Demetra noticed that the ray of sunshine also illuminated the golden corners of an old and tattered book. The book looked very valuable. She could tell that the book was very old because the pages were a dingy, dirty brown. There were cracks all through the leather binding. The title was also golden and looked like 'EL....something' or other. She just couldn't see the whole title.... SUDDENLY, the hair on her arms stood straight up! A tingle ran down her spine, her ears started buzzing as if she had just been jolted with an electric shock. Her heart started hammering in her chest, and her mind began to race! What was the matter with her? What's going on she wondered? Why did just looking at that book make her feel so strange? What is Mr. Kirk doing with something that looks so valuable, and what's he up to with the rush on this field trip? It was so unlike him to spring a field trip on them with hardly any notice. He was always so reserved. Everything was always so well planned. Last year when our class went to the caverns, we knew a month and a half a head of time about it, and we had three weeks to return our signed permission slips. This time, he's only giving us a couple of days to return them.

# Chapter 2
# The Willow

As they walked home after school Demetra asked, "Charlie, did you see that book Mr. Kirk had in his satchel?" "No, I am afraid I didn't. Why?" he asked. "*Charlie*, when I looked at that book, it was like it was glowing or something. I felt really weird when I looked it. I couldn't even make out the whole title before I got this buzzing in my ears; I got *goose bumps* on my arms! I'm telling you Charlie it was *really* weird!" exclaimed Demetra "Don't you think it was just a little bit strange that Mr. Kirk decided to take the class on a field trip, right out of the blue?" asked Demetra "And, he is only giving us until Friday to turn in the permission slips!" "I have to say that was a bit unusual for him Demetra. He is always so organized. I wonder what he is up to," Charlie said. "I don't know, but I want to get to the bottom of it. He is so weird sometimes, it *really* is hard to figure him out!" exclaimed Demetra As they approached their homes, Charlie asked Demetra if she wanted him to come hang out with her but Demetra really just wanted to be alone so she could gather her thoughts and try to piece together the day's events. So she just replied "Not today Charlie. Dad has a list of things for me to do around the farm and I'm sure mom has added some chores since I left for school this morning." "Are you sure? I can help," Charlie said. "No, I think I can handle it but, thanks anyway," Demetra replied. So with that Charlie headed for home and Demetra was finally alone. But instead of going home she decided to go sit under the willow to collect her thoughts. The willow was a very old tree that had been on her family's farm since before her grandfather was born. She could remember as a little girl going there, and imagining that she could see the face of a kindly old man in its scaly bark. She would stay there for hours and talk to the tree just like it was her very best friend. Demetra still loved to go there and just lie under its branches. She would watch as the branches, full of leaves; swayed back and forth while listening to the birds singing their sweet songs. Of course right now, the weeping branches were almost bare, but that didn't make it any less beautiful. The willow was just beginning to get the soft lime green color of its new spring coat. She ducked under its golden-yellow branches and threw her book bag between two huge roots making it into a comfortable makeshift pillow, as she always did. She lay down and got comfortable. Demetra closed her eyes and just as she was starting to let her mind wander... "OUCH"! Something bit her! Right on the very end of her nose! Demetra jumped up and looked around to see what it could have been. It wasn't even spring yet! Bugs were not supposed to be out! Just then, she noticed what appeared to be a ..... *leaf*.... zoom past her eyes. She jumped back only to find it zipping past her face again! Demetra swatted at it but that only *made things worse*. The leaf began to flutter like a hummingbird right in front of her face. Demetra began to get a clear view of a tiny face. There was a tiny body in the center of the leaf. As the creature stretched out its arms it took the shape of a full bright green leaf that had just fallen from the tree. But wait…that couldn't be! There weren't any leaves on the tree yet! ZOOM…The creature lashed out at her again! *This time*…it took the time to stop! Dead center! Right between her eyes! It was if the creature wanted her to take a good, look! A really *close* look! What she saw baffled her. "What…ah...ah…who are you?" Demetra asked. The creature looked like a tiny human, camouflaged as a leaf. "My name is TILLY! And… I – am - a - LEAF SPRITE!" the creature exclaimed, with its fists on its hips… and a *real* attitude! "And us leaf sprites **do not** take kindly to *anything* harming our plants, our flowers or, in your case, our homes. *Your big butt* just crushed my brand new hut! Now what am I supposed to do?" "I..I..I..I am so sorry,"

Demetra stuttered not believing that she was actually having a full conversation with a 'leaf sprite' and *understanding* what it was saying to her at that! "I..I..I.. can help fix it," she expressed. "I…I… what! Cat claw got your tongue!" Tilly asked. "N…No, I…I just, I mean, I…I can't believe that you exist! Creatures like you only exist in story books, and in dreams." "Yes, well, that just goes to show that there is a lot that you blasted humans don't know! A lot you *do not* understand!" Tilly said in that smart little voice of hers, zipping back and forth in front of my face again…just like a hummingbird… a really *mad* hummingbird! "But maybe we could understand," Demetra said "if only you would show us. Tilly please; calm down, would you just calm down Tilly! Not all of us humans are bad, I'm certainly not." Tilly slowly began to calm herself down… *finally*. "I'm sorry," Tilly explained. "It is just that here lately the whole wood has been on edge. The whole world is currently in turmoil. We leaf sprites are usually safe in our hidden meadows but since our realm is now in darkness it has forced us to search other realms in which to be safe. That's why I am in your realm." "I don't understand," Demetra said. "What do you mean my realm, your realm, and other realms?" "Urrrr! Humans! Don't they teach you *anything* in school these days?" Tilly said sarcastically "Let me start from the beginning. The world that you know is made up of four elements, Earth, Air, Fire, and Water. All four of these elements are needed in order for the world to exist. Each element has its own realm, and its own King or Queen. The King or Queen of each realm takes care of all the creatures that live there. Each realm can only be entered through a hidden portal somewhere on our planet. Humans virtually walk around being our neighbors but don't even know we are present. My realm is Eden. The evil sorcerer Tagu has found the Book of 'El' and plans to unleash Cronus at the beginning of the spring solstice which, I am afraid, is only in a week's time. He has captured one of the Elementals, Gaia;

she is the Queen of the Eden realm. She is the controller of the Earth Element. Tagu has created a massive Mortar army to aid him is his battle to free Cronus so Cronus can take over the world again. We magical creatures have had to flee and find a safe haven elsewhere, outside of Eden, that's why you are now able to see and understand me," explained Tilly. "Who is Cronus and why is he trying to take over?" Demetra asked. "Cronus is the father of all the Elementals. His children, the Elemental Kings and Queens, imprisoned him because he was ruling the world in a vile and wicked way. Now Tagu, the evil sorcerer, is plotting to free Cronus from his imprisonment. I am afraid that it is only a matter of time before the world as we know it falls and everyone, humans included, will fall under Cronus' rule. The only ones who can imprison Cronus are the direct descendants of the Elementals, which; to you humans would be Cronus' grandchildren. They hold the key to imprison him to the depths of hell where he should never be able to escape again. The problem is that no one knows where the children are except for, their parents, the Elemental Gods. They hid their children on earth at birth and disguised them so they would be safe from the evil Cronus. Only the Decedents have the power, when combined and seated at the ancient stone table, to put an end to Cronus and his reign of terror. For the Elemental Kings and Queens bestowed their powers onto their children at birth. Their full powers are only available to them when the death of their parents takes place. That leaves the Elemental Kings and Queens themselves powerless against Cronus. That's the price that is paid when the Elemental Gods choose to have children; after all they have to have an heir. Unfortunately, Tagu just recently released Malik who is the commander of the Mortar army and together they grow stronger and stronger each day. If Tagu is not stopped he will find the children, the Descendants, capture them, and release Cronus to take over the world," explained Tilly. "But how can we find them if no one knows where they are but the Elementals?" asked Demetra "DDUUHH…...." said Tilly under her breath. "We have to find the Elementals." "So how do we find the Elementals then the Descendants, miss smarty pants, excuse me miss smarty leaf?" Demetra asked, giving Tilly a little bit of attitude herself. "All four of the children have been hidden around the world, and no one knows their location or the location of their parents. But; there is rumor that 'The Man in the Willow' holds the clues to find the Elementals. He lives in the center of the willow," Tilly replied. "This willow?" Demetra questioned. "Yes, this willow…you humans *really are* slow to catch on, aren't you," Tilly stated. "Only he can give you the information that you seek. But be warned! He can be grumpy; so be sure to ask only good questions for he will not tolerate any nonsense," explained Tilly. "There is **no way** he could be grumpier that you are…. never mind Tilly…sorry I said that. So, how do I get to see him?" Demetra asked. "Just sit back and watch but remember; you only get one chance so you better make it a good question." Tilly centered her finger in the middle of the tree. As her finger touched the bark, the tree began to illuminate a golden color…kind of like pixie dust. She traced a circle on the bark and as she completed the circle and lifted her finger, the craggy face of an ancient man began to appear from the tree. "Why do you disturb me on this day?" said a grumpy voice. Demetra stared into the green eyes of a weathered old face made of silvery gray bark. Demetra knew that he was aged with wisdom, but she could see softness in his eyes. "I am very sorry to disturb you sir, my name is Demetra Scott and I need to know how I can find the Descendants?" "Only the Elementals can tell you that!" The Man in the Willow bellowed. "You must seek out the book of 'EL'! It will be your guide to find the Elementals, for they are the only ones who know the location of their children. You must also know that in order for the Elementals to give you the location of their descendants they will have to offer their lives. For their souls are the *only* maps to their children!" A light went off in Demetras head! "I have seen that book!" she exclaimed "My teacher Mr. Kirk had it shoved in his satchel today during class as he discussed our upcoming field trip to Stonehenge." "Be very careful Demetra Scott," The Man in the Willow warned, "for if that book were to fall into the wrong hands, there is no telling what devastation would be unleashed upon this whole planet." "Yes sir, I will get the book and keep it safe. Thank you for your help," Demetra replied respectfully to The Man in the Willow, as his ancient face disappeared back into the bark of the old willow tree.

# Chapter 3
# Convincing Charlie

On the way home Demetra wondered if she should try to explain to Charlie all that had just taken place at the willow. Would he understand? It was hard enough for her to understand it…and she had been there! Or would he just think that she was plum crazy? She never kept anything from Charlie. He was like her right hand. Trying to keep this from him would probably be much more stressful than telling him about it. It was best if she just went right now, told Charlie everything, and then together they would try to solve the problem. That's exactly what she would do. She would go see Charlie and tell him about it while everything was still fresh in her mind! Demetras father had made a shortcut through the corn field, so she and Charlie could cut through to each other's homes quicker. She took the shortcut now. Once she arrived, she found Charlie in the barn picking his mare's hoof. Charlie eased the mare's hoof down and slowly stood up, cracking nearly every bone in his back. He gave the horse a few loving strokes, scratched her behind her ears then turned to Demetra and smiled, "Change your mind on that help?" he asked. "Not really Charlie. Listen! I need you to sit down. There is something important that I need to talk with you about." Demetra said mysteriously. Charlie removed his brown leather gloves and tossed them onto a nearby bale of straw. He grabbed a milking bucket, turned it upside down and took a seat. "Yes ma'am, I'm all ears. So, what's going on Demetra? Are you alright? What's all the fuss?" "Charlie, instead of going home to help my father like I said, I decided to go to the willow. I know, I know; I told you I have work to do, and I do, but I just needed time to clear my head and gather my thoughts," she said. "But I thought that you had tons of chores to do at home," Charlie said. "Yes!" Demetra exclaimed. "I do have chores to do at home but; I have *really* been having a hard time wrapping my head around all that's been going on, you know, the weird dreams and everything. Sorry, I just needed some time alone, to think. Anyway, as I got comfortable under the willow; I was bitten right on the end of my nose and then yelled at by a leaf sprite who then introduced me to The Man of the Willow. Who then said we *must* get that book Mr. Kirk had in his satchel, you know the book I told you made me feel so weird. Then the leaf sprite, whose name Tilly she informed me in no uncertain terms, went on to tell me that our realm of the world is taken care of and was created by four gods who are called Elementals. They control the different realms of the world; Earth, Air, Fire, and Water. She said that just recently, an evil sorcerer, named Tagu, released the commander of the Mortar army whose name is Malik, and together they are trying to release Cronus who is the father of the Elementals. Years ago the Elementals, Cronus' children, imprisoned Cronus because he was ruling the world in an evil manner. Tilly and The Man in the Willow said that if Tagu is allowed to unleash Cronus, together they will take over all of the realms, and Cronus will rule the entire world! We have to help save them Charlie, we just have to! Will you help me?" Charlie sat on his bucket with his mouth gaped wide open in total disbelief. "Whoa. I don't know what to say Demetra. *Do you really* expect me to believe something like that? I mean really Demetra, a leaf sprite, different realms of the world, evil sorcery, Elementals...Really? And, what in the world does Mr. Kirk's dumb old book have to do with any of this?" Shocked by what Charlie said, Demetra's face turned ten shades of red "Now you listen to me Charlie O'Conner! You have known me all of your life! ALL OF YOUR LIFE! Have I EVER lied to you, made up bull-crap stories, or treated you crossly in any way possible?" Demetra shouted angrily. "Well.... I suppose not." Charlie said quietly. "It's not *you* I don't believe Demetra. All this just sounds…ummmm…kind of…ummm...farfetched." "I'm telling you Charlie, this…just…happened…to…me!" she exclaimed. "The Man of the Willow and Tilly said we can't let Tagu get Mr. Kirks book, we have to get it, and we can't let Tagu and Malik release Cronus!" "Okay, so what if for a second I believe all this crazy stuff? What can you and I possibly do?"

# Chapter 4
# Mr. Kirk

The next morning Charlie and Demetra decided that not only did they have to try and figure out what Mr. Kirk was up to, but they needed to get their hands on that book! "Demetra; Mr. Kirk is not stupid!" said Charlie "If that book is as important as we think it is then he is not going to leave it lying around just anywhere." "It's not just about the book Charlie! We need to figure out what he is up to," exclaimed Demetra. As they approached their classroom they noticed Mr. Kirk had already arrived at school. There he was; sitting at his desk tapping his foot impatiently and jotting down notes in his notebook. "Ahhhh, nice to see you both, did you have a nice evening?" "Sure," they both said together. "Well hurry then and take your seats. We have a very important lesson today." As Demetra took her seat, she took a good hard look at Mr. Kirk's desk to see if she could catch a glimpse of his satchel or, more importantly, the book. It was nowhere to be found. Hmm she thought; I wonder if it is in his desk drawer. "Pssst, Charlie" Demetra whispered. "I don't see the book or the satchel anywhere; it must be in his desk drawer. We need to think of a diversion." "I got it," Charlie said. "We wait until we are on the way to lunch, I will fall down and act like I twisted my ankle. As Mr. Kirk is tending to me, you sneak back to the classroom and take a peek to see if it's there. If it is there, grab it and hide it, we will retrieve it after lunch. Mr. Kirk will not even know it's missing until after school has let out." After all of the students arrived for class Mr. Kirk rushed them to their seats as well. "Hurry class! We have a lot to get to today so it's best we get started right away. Due to our upcoming field trip, I thought it might be a good idea if we take the time to learn a little history about our destination." Mr. Kirk pulled out a pictured sketch of the circular formation of stones and taped it to the chalk board. "Every one of you has heard of Stonehenge correct?" Mr. Kirk asked. "Well, it has been said, that there is actually, a very different side to Stonehenge. A side that is not talked about so much, a side filled with myth and legend. Everyone knows that the world is made up of the common four elements Earth, Air, Fire and Water. For centuries, the best historians and archeologists, from all over the world, have never been able to actually tell the origins of Stonehenge ...... Right? So what if I asked you, for just a moment, to open your mind to other ideas as to the origins of Stonehenge. What would you say then class? What if I said that the purposes, of the four pillar stone archways are actually doorways into the different realms of Earth, Wind, Fire and Water? And that the fifth archway, which is at the head of the circle, could be opened up to reveal the heavens. What would you say to that class?" Suddenly a girl with long blonde pigtails raised her hand and waited anxiously to be called upon by Mr. Kirk. It was none other than Miss Abigail Ross. She was one of the most popular girls at West Edwards Jr. High School. Her parents were one of the wealthiest couples in Wickets Hollow. She was always trying to score brownie points with every teacher at school. I think that she may even have a bit of a crush on my good old friend Charlie. "Yes, Miss Ross?" Mr. Kirk asked. "Mr. Kirk, if all of these things you are saying are true why hasn't anyone ever talked about it before? I mean…what makes you think this particular theory is true?" "Good question Ms. Ross. Although this theory has not been proven, and I might add, no other theory has been proven to be true either, this theory is usually only discussed in certain circles. Most experts discredit this theory. There are only a select few, me included, that believe in the *real* origins of this planet." Abigail seemed to be content with Mr. Kirk's answer. She sat back in her chair and gave Demetra a snotty little grin. Demetra just shook her head, rolled her eyes and raised her hand. "Yes

24

Miss Scott?" he acknowledged her hand being raised. "Mr. Kirk, how do you know for sure that all you have just told us today is the truth? I guess what I am trying to ask is what proof do you have, that this theory is indeed correct?" "Well! If proof is what you want, then proof is what you will get!" he said angrily, and with that statement, he strutted around his desk, like a little bantam rooster, reached into the desk drawer and pulled out the same leather book she had seen in his satchel yesterday. He stuck it straight up in the air victoriously! Only this time she could take a good look at the whole book and it was indeed labeled the book of 'EL'. Oh no! She could not believe it! She was getting that weird feeling again! The book had such a mysterious presence to it. "This is your proof Miss Scott!" Mr. Kirk exclaimed as he waved it around. "It is all in here! This explains the way the world *really* began. I have searched the world over and I finally have the proof I need to show everyone that *my* theory is correct!" Just as the word correct left his lips…the bell rang for lunch. "Finally," Demetra said as she met with Charlie at the classroom door. "Are you ready?" Charlie asked nervously. Together they walked down the hallway. When they reached the corner Charlie, as if he was in horrible pain, fell to his bottom and held his ankle. "OW! OW! OW!" he groaned. As everyone gathered around him trying to catch a glimpse of what was going on, Demetra slipped out through the back of the crowd and rushed back to the classroom unnoticed. When she reached the classroom, she quickly tried to open the desk drawer but she found it was locked. "Dang it!" she muttered to herself. She remembered that she always kept a hairpin in her bag for her hair; maybe she could pick the lock with it she thought. Quickly she rustled through her bag and finally found the pin. She zipped up her bag, and as she stood up…….. she was met face to face by none other than Mr. Kirk himself. His face was dead level with hers. "Forget something Miss Scott?" he asked Demetras' heart was beating like a drum. "I…I…ahh… just forgot my hairpin

25

Mr. Kirk," she said shakily. "Hmm," Mr. Kirk said curiously. "Well, you had best get to lunch. It seems that your friend Charlie is just fine." "Yes sir," she said as she put her head down and headed for the door. Mr. Kirk stopped her and said "Demetra; don't you need to put your hair up with your pin?" "Oh! Y…yes sir, sorry," and as she walked away she quickly placed her hair back with the pin. She soon met up with Charlie in the cafeteria "*Where have you been!*" Charlie asked "I was so worried. I tried to hold him off but he had one of the other students stay with me while he went to fetch the nurse." "He caught me Charlie; well kind of. The dang drawer was locked! So, I grabbed a hair pin from my bag so I could try to pick the lock and he walked right up behind me!" exclaimed Demetra. "I think he knew Demetra," Charlie said in a worried tone. "I think you're right Charlie. That was a close one. But how are we supposed to get the book now? If we don't get the book of 'EL' Tilly and The Man in the Willow said we are all doomed!" cried Demetra. "We will just have to follow him tonight and see if we can get it then," said Charlie gently.

# Chapter 5
# The Book

After school Demetra and Charlie decided to hide in the bushes just outside
of the school yard where they could see Mr. Kirks bike. As he made his exit
from the main entrance of the school, they could see the satchel hanging from
his left shoulder. Mr. Kirk walked bristly to his bike, threw his leg over and
started down the road toward his home. They watched as he pedaled through
the school gates. Demetra and Charlie followed him unnoticed hiding behind
the trees and bushes until finally arriving at a small cottage set back on a dark
lane. The lane was lined with tall, stately oak trees. The home itself was very
old. It was made of wood and was painted white with black trim. The outside
was very un-kept, weeds and wild flowers grew abundantly. Clearly he had
let the yard go to seed. It looked as if it had not been mowed in decades. The
two friends hid behind a tall hedge row on the side of the cottage. They
watched as Mr. Kirk parked his bike and walked inside the house. "What do
we do now Demetra?" Charlie whispered. "We wait, that's what," she replied
quietly. As night fell, Demetra began to think that they were not ever going to
get a chance to get a peek inside. The lights were on all over the house. All of
a sudden; the lights turned off. All at once! Except for one…at the side of the
house there was one light left on but it was very dim and was sort of a light
green color, kind of creepy looking. Demetra and Charlie decided sneak up
to the window to see if they could catch a glimpse of what was going on inside.
They tiptoed steadily to the edge of the glass and peeked through the window.
They could not believe what their eyes were seeing! There was Mr. Kirk;
standing behind a tall wooden podium with a goofy looking hat on his head.
At school he was always so refined. On top of the podium they saw the book,

lying wide open. Mr. Kirk was studying the pages carefully, turning them one by one. On a long wooden table beside him was a beautiful tall, shiny silver bowl. The bowl was surrounded by dozens of glass bottles. The bottles were different colors, all the colors of the rainbow, and they looked like jewels sparkling in the sunlight. They were filled with cloudy liquids, and some looked like they had herbs in them. Slowly; one by one he began to pour the ingredients, from different bottles, into the shiny silver bowl. The room began to illuminate a glowing, eerie neon green color and bright purple smoke began to fill the air. Suddenly, the smoke cleared and the light changed back to the creepy light green. In the center of the room, in the middle of the dark wooden floor was a huge circle. It appeared to have been drawn with chalk. Inside the circle was a cross that separated the circle into four different sections. Each section had a different marking, making it look like some sort of diagram. Without saying a word Mr. Kirk picked up the shiny silver bowl. He walked slowly around the table and ceremoniously poured the liquid from it into the center of the diagram. Immediately where Mr. Kirk had poured the liquid, a strange shimmering pool began to form. The liquid now seemed to be clear as if it were water, not cloudy at all. Slowly, a tall human shape began to form and rise up out of the shimmering pool of liquid, crystal blue water ran flowing from all its sides. It looked like it was a human waterfall. Mr. Kirk began to have a conversation with it. "I can't hear a blasted thing from out here Charlie," Demetra whispered. "Let's sneak around the house, maybe we can find a way inside." When they reached the front of the house they were both quite shocked to find the front door unlocked! Charlie twisted the knob and cracked the door open just enough so they could both squeeze through. Quietly they entered Mr. Kirks home and found themselves in complete darkness. The only thing they could see was the glowing green light that seeped eerily from the cracks around the door at the end of the hall. "That's it Demetra! There's the room," whispered Charlie. The two of them tiptoed quietly to the end of the hallway; Charlie kneeled down on both knees and peeked through the keyhole, while Demetra bent over him trying to peer through the cracks around the door. "I know master. Everything is in place. They will soon find their way to us, and we will have them all at once," Mr. Kirk assured the watery form. "I am running out of time and patience **DO NOT** disappoint me!" said the watery form, in a deep vibrating voice that made the wooden floor under Charlie and Demetras feet tremble. "My army is at hand waiting. I REPEAT, DO NOT DISAPPOINT ME!" "It will be as you wish master," Mr. Kirk said. Then, just as quickly as it had appeared, the waterfall formation depleted itself back into the floor and disappeared, as if it were never there. Suddenly, all of the lights came back on! "Demetra, we have to hide! He is going to come out and catch us," Charlie whispered nervously. Demetra turned around and noticed a huge sofa placed in the room opposite them. "Quick Charlie! Behind the sofa." They both crawled quickly and quietly to the sofa and hid behind it. Slowly, the door at the end of the hall opened…and out walked Mr. Kirk removing the bow tie from around his neck. They, peeked around the sofa, waited patiently and watched as Mr. Kirk walked from room to room fiddling, cleaning, and turning off the lights as he left each room. He visited the water closet and came back wearing a long nightgown that dragged along the floor as he walked. They watched him walk into his bedroom, turn back the covers and *finally* climb into his bed. He turned off his bedside lamp; he was in bed for the night…they hoped! AT LAST they heard gentle snores coming from Mr. Kirks' bedroom. Slowly they crawled out from behind the sofa and started creeping toward the hallway, hoping no boards would creak and give them away. They made their way cautiously down the hallway toward the room where they hoped the book still was. When they reached the room they found that the door was wide open. On all fours they continued creeping into the room. They gently closed the door enough so they could use the flashlight to see but; to be sure that Mr. Kirk could not. After turning on the flashlight they were shocked at what they found. The diagram that had been drawn on the floor was completely gone! The floor wasn't even wet, not even damp! All of the beautiful colored vials were still on the table, as was the big silver bowl. Then, there on the podium was the book …still lying wide open to the page last used. Demetra flagged the page by pulling the ribbon from her hair and placing it in the book as she gently closed it. Holding the book tightly against her chest she signaled Charlie that it was time to get the heck out of there. Once they were out of Mr. Kirk's house, Demetra asked Charlie what he thought about all they had seen. "I don't know Demetra, but I will tell you this, I don't understand any of it. This is all crazy to me! Liquid formation beings, leaf sprites, old men in trees, Elemental Kings and Queens, Descendants, old enchanted books. I just don't know, I'm trying to take it all with a grain of salt." "Yes it is quite crazy but like it or not Charlie it's taking place and we have to help. Let's get home and get some sleep Mr. Kirk won't know the book is missing until tomorrow morning and we need to rest." With that the two friends headed for their homes…but more importantly their beds.

# Chapter 6
# Missing

Before she knew it, it was morning and Demetra awoke feeling very tired. She had gotten hardly any sleep last night. She wanted to get downstairs, before her mother had the chance to yell for her. She quickly got dressed and headed down for breakfast. To her amazement her parents were nowhere to be found. Breakfast had not even been prepared. She searched everywhere that she could think of but nothing. Demetra also ran down to the barn to see if her parents were out there. Usually if a calf was being born, her parents would be out there to make sure everything went smoothly with its birth. Nothing, they were not there either. She headed thru the cornfield short cut toward Charlie's house to see if her parents were there with Mr. O'Connor. She met Charlie in the middle of the shortcut, "I can't find my father anywhere Demetra!" Charlie exclaimed. "My parents are gone too Charlie!" Demetra said frantically. "I don't know what's going on. Let's go back to my house and see if we can find anything. Surely they just didn't disappear." When they arrived back at Demetras home they walked directly into the kitchen. They searched the room for clues as to what may have happened, but nothing. Charlie suggested they take a look out in the fields before they really panicked. Demetra asked Charlie to wait a minute, she told him she needed to go upstairs to get her satchel, but more importantly….the book. When she got to her bedroom door she found a note tacked to it that said her parents had gone into town. She grabbed her satchel and skipped down the stairs to tell Charlie that his father was probably with her parents, in town. As they headed out of the kitchen, Demetra noticed there was a long shiny black feather stuck to the wall. The tip of the feather was incased in metal making it as sharp as an icepick. Stuck under the sharp pointed tip was an elegant old looking piece of paper, embossed with jet black ink that read simply "BRING ME THE BOOK!" Demetra asked Charlie "How could Mr. Kirk know *we* have the book?"

# Chapter 7
# Wrens

SUDDENLY, a loud blood curdling screech echoed its way throughout the house bouncing off the walls as it hurled its way toward them. It was followed by another screech and another. The screeches were horrific, they sounded as if someone was raking their fingernails down a chalkboard and the sound was intensified by a million decibels. The screeches were so sharp and piercing it felt as if a blade had punctured their eardrums. Demetra and Charlie both had to cover their ears as they ran outside. When they got outside, the wind was howling like a banshee. It nearly whipped them off their feet it was so strong. It was like a twister had suddenly made an appearance right outside the door! The sky had turned dark gray with big billowing clouds overshadowing the sun. They ran quickly for Demetras fathers tractor and hunkered down in-between the two back wheels. She looked up from under the tractor to see hundreds of what seemed to be large crow like birds circling around and around, overhead. The creatures began to fly closer and closer and that's when Demetra noticed that they were no ordinary birds. She could not believe what she was seeing. The creatures were iridescent black; their blue-black wings were longer than any other bird known to man. Their legs were the tawny gold of a lion and their claws were as sharp as an eagle's talon. But; what was most fascinating was they were human from the waist up. Not just any human, an old human! Their faces looked as old as you would think Methuselahs would have looked. They were craggy and lined with wrinkles. Their heads were covered with long, stringy, scraggly gray hair. They had to be the scariest things she had ever laid eyes upon. "Charlie we need to get out of here! What are we going to do?" Just then the creatures began to swoop in, lower and lower, trying to grasp them with every swoop. Charlie let out a loud painful scream as one of the creatures dug its razor sharp claws into his leg! The creature had a hold on him and was dragging him out from under the tractor! Charlie was fighting the creature with everything he had. He was kicking, screaming and punching at its face. Suddenly, a brilliant flash of lighting arced across and lit up the whole dark sky, searing the windswept trees and everything immediately turned quiet. You could have heard a pin drop it was so quiet. It was if the whole world had stopped abruptly in its tracks. Demetra crawled out from under the tractor to see what was going on; she looked up and saw what appeared to be a large black horse emerging from the dark clouds above her. The horse was huge and as black as midnight. It ran toward them on eight legs instead of the normal four. Demetra could only look on in amazement as the horse approached her. Was it there to help them or, like the bird creatures, to harm her? She and Charlie had been through so much it was hard for her to recognize good from evil she thought. She was wondering whether to run or dive back under the tractor so it took her a second to realize that she was face to face with the horse. The scary thing was that apparently…she could speak horse … because she understood perfectly when the horse said to her frantically "Get on, hurry!" So Demetra jumped on the horses back. With one of its eight legs, it kicked the horrible bird creature making it release Charlie, at the same time the horse grabbed Charlie's tattered shirt in its mouth and threw him up onto its long sleek back beside Demetra. The horse darted off into the dark sky running on air. It wasn't long before the sun was setting at their backs and as the horse continued to head east it seemed the glowing silver moon was his guide. It was amazing to feel the cool night air flowing on their faces. It was cold back at home, way down below her, but up here it was just a bit cool. Cool, like your mother's hand touching your hot forehead when you have a high fever. Demetra took a deep breath and relaxed with a sigh. It was as if she were cradled in her mother's loving arms. She felt protected, she was finally at ease. "Who are you? Where are you taking us?" Demetra asked softly. "I am Turr," he said. "Those nasty creatures were Wrens. They were sent here by Tagu; no doubt he has caught wind of your scent. Our only option is to hide, we must keep the book safe at all costs or I'm afraid that all will be lost. I was sent by Queen Gaia to help you on your quest. You both should try and get some sleep." Demetra snuggled next to Charlie on Turrs wide warm back and while staring at the moon, quickly fell asleep.

# Chapter 8
# Atlantis

Demetra woke up to Turr nuzzling her shoulder. "We are approaching our destination," Turr said to Charlie and Demetra. "Where are we?" Charlie asked. "Nearing Atlantis," Turr replied. A blank expression came across the two friends faces as they gazed upon an extremely large glass dome filled with water. Atlantis? How could they be near Atlantis? They were clearly flying through space. They could actually see Earth below them. "It's been said that Atlantis disappeared into the ocean Turr; how could it be in space?" "Atlantis did not disappear under the ocean as you humans believe. King Poseidon had it lifted from the ocean to hide it from Cronus and his army who seek to demolish the great city. The stone fragments that humans have found are just the foundation of what was once the great city." As they flew closer and closer to Atlantis, Demetra began to get very nervous. It seemed as if Turr was going to fly right into the wall of the dome. Demetra let out a loud shriek as Turr whisked them straight through the dome. You see, Atlantis didn't have a *glass dome* it was made of water. "Wow, now that was awesome!" exclaimed Charlie. As they flew up above the city, they gazed in disbelief, and they couldn't help feeling overwhelmed with amazement. The city was huge and breathtakingly beautiful. It was highlighted with tranquil, emerald green lagoons and clear, sparkling aquamarine pools. Flowing effortlessly from the tall stone walls were beautiful cascading waterfalls. Demetra and Charlie had never seen anything so mesmerizing. There were statues carved throughout the stone pillars. They were covered in gold and precious metals, encrusted with jewels. Demetra heard a sniffle and looked over to find a tear coming from Charlie's eye. "What!" he said "It's so beautiful and peaceful." Residing in the center of the great city atop a hill, sat a large roman type palace. Standing tall in front of the palace was a carved white marble statue of Poseidon. He was standing in a golden carriage pulled by four winged horses. "Where are all the people?" she asked Charlie. "I know Demetra; the city is like a ghost town," he replied. Turr swooped in to land at the bottom of the steps; by the looks of the steps they had quite a walk ahead of them. After Demetra and Charlie climbed down off of Turr's back, there was a sudden blinding white hot shimmer of light that gleamed off of his sleek hide. The light was so bright that the two friends had to cover their eyes with their forearms. As the light faded Demetra looked into the eyes of not a horse, but a young man. A handsome young man who had the brightest, bluest eyes she had ever seen. His silky black hair flowed effortlessly with the breeze. "Turr," Demetra asked "is that you?" "Sorry Demetra with all of the confusion I was unable to tell you that I'm a shape shifter. I am able to take any form. I mostly try to stay human but; sometimes things change," replied Turr with a shrug of his shoulder. Out of nowhere Charlie jumped into the conversation with a bit of an attitude. "Don't you think it would be wise to tell people these types of things, it's not every day that you meet up with a shape shifter?" Turr took a step forward, toward Charlie and said "I didn't see you complaining when I was saving your butt from the Wrens." Demetra shook her head and said "Boy's, boy's let's remember why we are here! By the way Turr, what are we doing here?" "You must petition King Poseidon to grant you the location of his daughter. If not, we will not be heading off to a good start in saving the world." With Charlie and Turr in tow, Demetra turned and began to walk up the stairs toward the palace entrance. Once they reached the top of the stairs they were greeted by two men, Brandeis blue sort of an ocean blue, in color with definite fish like characteristics. Noticeably on their necks were gills and in between their toes were webbed. They were wearing emerald green leather armor. In one hand they held a golden shield which was engraved with Poseidon's Trident. The other hand held tall metal staffs that were sharply forked at the ends. Fins jetted from their back as they turned to open the double doors. Demetra lead them through the threshold to find that the room was full of Atlanteans, in all shapes, colors and sizes. Fish featured mothers; fathers and children lined the room trying to catch a glimpse of them. The friends pushed forward making their way up to the front of the room. They stood at the bottom of steps which led up to a platform made of stone outlined in gold. Sitting on top of the platform was a giant golden chair encrusted with beautiful gems and rare stones. Behind the chair was a coral reef brimming with plant life of all shapes and colors. Suddenly, huge shiny brass trumpets began to sound loudly, announcing, Poseidon himself. He walked regally out from behind sapphire colored satin curtains that lined the back portion of the platform. They could feel his presence when he entered the room, it was thick with power. He walked with the utmost confidence. His face aged with wisdom and his body riddled with battle scars. He took his seat and gazed upon them with the darkest, most disdainful look she had ever encountered. Demetra shrank into her skin and gulped as she gathered her nerve enough to speak. "We are terribly sorry to have bothered you your highness but;" Poseidon quickly interrupted her with a voice as loud as thunder, vibrating the whole room. "I know why you are here and the answer is **NO!**" "Why should I give you the location of my beloved daughter? For what, Cronus? Ha! **I think not!** Cronus stands no chance to penetrate these walls. I refuse to put Atlanteans or my precious daughter in jeopardy." Poseidon's voice had reached every ear in the room. "Your highness please," Demetra pleaded. "You must understand it's not just Atlantis that will need your help it's the whole world that Cronus seeks rule. His revenge will have no mercy on any of us!" Poseidon's face grew deep dark red with anger. "How *dare* you defy me!" he thundered. "*I* fear no one! If it's a war Cronus wants then it's a war he will get! Vows were taken when the children were born! All the Elementals know that the children are not to be put at risk!" Angrily Poseidon got up and stormed regally out of the room leaving the three friends open mouthed with shock. The great hall began to fill with whispers and quiet talks. "We should find a place to stay overnight, and get a game plan together," Turr explained. As they headed for the door that led out of the great hall, they felt surrounded. There were thousands of eyes watching them, hungrily, as if they were worms on a hook at the end of a fishing pole. They did *not* want to be fish bait! They felt very uncomfortable so they quickly hit the cobblestone paved roads in search of a place to stay for the night. During their search, they stumbled upon a building with a young Atlantean at the front. "Pssst!" She motioned for them to come closer. Whispering, she explained to them that they could stay there for the night but must leave before day break. The young woman led the three friends up the stairs to a small room with a bed and seat. Once inside it didn't take Charlie long to pass out. It had been a long couple of days, but she wasn't ready to sleep yet. She walked out and leaned over the stone balcony. Amazing, she thought as she gazed out over a beautiful emerald green lagoon. The setting sunlight sparkled on its rippling surface, making it shine like diamonds. There were three beautiful mermaids lying on some rocks at the edge of the lagoon. Their turquoise scales twinkled like jewels in the sunshine. Several more mermaids were playing and splashing happily in the emerald green water. It was a beautiful sight. Still, she couldn't help wondering what she was going to do. She had traveled so far and had risked not only her life, but the life of her best friend as well. For them to have gotten to this point, only to be completely shut down by Poseidon so quickly, really upset Demetra. A hand gently squeezed and released her shoulder; it was Turr giving her a comforting touch. "Don't worry Demetra, we will find a way to persuade Poseidon into giving us the location of his daughter," Turr said gently. "How Turr?" Demetra pleaded. Turr grabbed both her shoulders with his hands. He spun her around and said "Look in my eyes Demetra, we *will* find a way to get the location of King Poseidon's daughter. You have to believe in yourself! Don't lose hope." Demetra didn't hear a word he said…she was lost in the beautiful blue of his eyes and her heart could not help but skip a beat!

# Chapter 9
# Booms in the night!

It seemed like Demetra had just gone to sleep when the whole building began to tremble and shake vigorously. It was as if they were suddenly besieged by an earthquake. Demetra stumbled out of bed only to trip over Charlie's sleeping corpse lying right smack dab in the middle of the room. Aggravated, she kicked Charlie in the leg. Waking up with a shout Charlie asked, "What the heck is the matter with you Demetra? What did you kick me for?" Demetra exclaimed, "Get up quick Charlie. Something is going on." They rushed out to the balcony; Turr had already beaten them there. Once outside it didn't take them long to realize that they were under attack. It was the Wrens again, only this time, they didn't come alone. Turr quickly informed them that unfortunately, there were Mortars clutched to the back of the Wrens. The beastly creatures were green in color but looked like they had just rolled around in a fire pit. They were covered with ash. Nasty, sharp yellow teeth protruded from their mouths, and saliva dripped down their chins. Clutched in their hands, were long staffs that sent streams of bright orange fireballs wherever it was aimed. Turr looked at Demetra and Charlie and exclaimed "We have to get to the palace!" Turr jumped up on the railing of the balcony and with a blinding flash he transformed himself into the horse again. He yelled to Demetra who was closest to his head. "Get on quickly! We have to get to King Poseidon! If they capture him we will never have the chance to find Amalta!" They jumped onto his back and in a split second Demetra and Charlie were slung off of it again, violently...only to land on a nearby rooftop. Sitting up shakily Demetra grabbed her head in pain. Blood dripped through her fingers. "Charlie!" she yelled, "Charlie where are you! Answer me! Turr!

Hello?" Finally, some of the smoke cleared and she saw the figure of a person lying at the other end of the rooftop. After crawling slowly to the figure, she found it was Charlie. Gently rolling him over, she put her ear to his chest to check for a heartbeat. Charlie began to cough. Carefully lifting his head up she said, "Charlie, are you okay? Please speak to me." He opened his eyes, looked at her and said "I'm fine. Are you okay?" "I'm okay, just a little cut on my head; but I can't find Turr," she said, her voice trembling. Getting to his feet Charlie looked over the edge of the roof to find Turr in the middle of the cobblestone street. "There he is Demetra! We have to get down there to help him before anything else bad happens." "How?" Demetra asked, "This place is crawling with Mortars and Wrens!" Whap! A stinging pain hit the back of Demetra's neck. "Ouch! What was that?" Whap! She grabbed the back of her neck; "Ouch!" there it was again. Demetra looked behind her to find a young boy throwing pebbles at her. "What, are you doing?" she yelled. "Grab my hands; I know a place where we can hide," the boy said. The minute Demetra and Charlie grabbed his scaly blue hands they were instantly whisked off the rooftop and found themselves standing beside Turr on the cobblestone street below. As his human body laid there, neon green blood had begun to pool beneath him. Extremely worried, she reached out to him and said. "Turr are you okay? Please speak to me." With a weak voice Turr said "I'm okay. It's just a little cut, that's all." "Why do guys always think they have to be so tough? Come on Turr, don't act like there's nothing wrong! You are acting like *such* a macho man. I know you're hurt, let's get you out of here." Pointing at their rescuer Demetra explained to Turr that the boy knew where they could hide for a little bit. With all their combined strength they lifted him as gently as possible. With one of Turrs arms around each of their necks they followed the young boy as he made his way down a dark alley only to stop at a stone wall at the end. "There's nothing here!" Demetra exclaimed "There's nothing here to you but; you're not from around here, now are you?" The young boy said with a smile. "Trust me," he said. He pulled a silver necklace from under his blue silk like shirt. Attached to the necklace was a small rectangular crystal. The boy took the crystal and held it against the stone wall. The necklace began to gleam streams of aqua blue light. The stone wall began to break away revealing a hidden passageway through a dark tunnel. Once they made it through the opening, the boy turned around and held his necklace up to the opening making the stones form back together again, hiding their entrance. Just as the stones were about to completely form together again, one of the Mortar soldiers rushed up to the doorway only to get his hand stuck in the forming stones. The hand started wiggling side to side, slashing back and forth trying to free itself from the stone wall. The boy walked over to the wall, grabbed a piece of seaweed that was growing there and started smacking the Mortars hand with it really aggravating it…it thrashed harder trying to get its hand out of the wall. "You thought you could follow us…didn't you." The boy said tauntingly. "Aughm, Aughm" Demetra cleared her throat and reminded them that they needed to push forward. "Man, I have *got* to get me one of those crystals things," Charlie said. The boy just grinned at him. As the friends walked down the dark path it was eerily quiet. Charlie decided that he would break the silence and ask the boy what his name was. "My name is Cree," the boy answered. "Okay Cree, nice to meet you. My name is Charlie, this is Demetra and our injured friend is Turr. By the way, where are you taking us?" asked Charlie. "Don't worry, it's safe down here. Your friend Turr will be able to rest, and mend," Cree said. "How can we rest when your whole world is under attack?" asked Charlie. "Don't worry Charlie; Atlanteans generally come out the victor in most battles," Cree said. "Anyway, we are headed to our healing room. Our people have come here for generations to heal the sick and tend to the wounded. These Crystals have marvelous healing powers. They will heal your leg, and they will heal your friend as well." The narrow passage way began to widen and opened into a cavern with enormous, beautiful sapphire blue crystal's jetting from the ground, the whole room and floor illuminated a shimmering light aquamarine blue color. "We will rest here for now," Cree explained "and you two can heal." As they all got comfortable Demetra couldn't resist asking Cree what he knew about the Princess Amalta, and if he might know where she was hidden. "I do not know where Princess Amalta resides; only the Elementals know. It is rumored that each Elemental King or Queen must *willingly* give up their lives and souls in order for their children to be found. It's said that this was the only way to insure that the children's safety would be assured." "So, how do we get to the palace Cree, we need to get to King Poseidon." Cree answered "I can take you but Turr is far too weak to go. What do you want to do?" Demetra replied, "I've got it, Charlie you stay here with Turr. Cree and I will go to the palace and find King Poseidon." Charlie didn't even hesitate; he said "No problem. I can handle it." Demetra turned to Turr and asked "Are you sure you will be okay?" Turr reached for her hand and with his hand holding hers he looked into her eyes and said "I will be here waiting for you."

# Chapter 10
# Frozen in Time

Cree again held his crystal necklace against the stone wall, this time forming a window. This allowed them to peer outside. They could easily see that Atlantis was in turmoil. Atlanteans were running through the streets screaming with fear. There were flames jetting from a number of different buildings. Demetra exclaimed, "We must get to King Poseidon!" Again Cree placed his crystal against the wall and a doorway was formed in the wall, allowing them to pass through. Cree turned around and closed the entrance back up behind them. Cree and Demetra sneaked through alleys and around corners. They ran along the dark side of the roads making sure to be as discreet as possible. The last thing they needed right now was to be caught by those ghastly Mortars. Once they reached the wall that surrounded the palace they took a moment to study just how they were going to plan their entrance. "There are Mortars and Wrens everywhere Cree!" Demetra whispered, "How are we going to get inside?" "Don't worry Demetra you have to be an Atlantean to think like one!" Cree whispered to her with a big grin. "This is what we are going to do. Once I create a diversion, you get quickly into the castle. You must stay low and hidden until I get there." "Please be careful Cree!" Demetra pleaded. "I'll see you soon," he replied. Demetra watched Cree as he yelled and shook his fist at the Mortars enticing them to chase him. As they chased Cree around the stone gates it was if Cree was swimming, quickly, in midair. This allowed Demetra to check to make sure that the coast was clear and she quickly rushed up the stairs. Once inside she crouched between the wall and a stone table that had been flipped onto its side and shoved against the wall. She placed both hands on the table edge and peered over the top of the table. She could see King Poseidon surrounded by Mortar soldiers. They were holding spears and swords to his chest and throat. Demetra could not believe what she was seeing, she knew that scar! She would recognize that scar and that horrible face anywhere! It was the same creature she had battled in her dreams! Its muscled forearms were encased to its wrists by worn, crimson red leather. Its ham size fists were propped on its hips arrogantly. Scratches and scars littered the creature's body as if it had been tortured for centuries. Demetra knew instantly, that *he* was the leader of the pack. Hidden behind the table she started to tremble. What in the world was she going to do now? It seemed that things had just gone from BAD to WORSE! She dropped her trembling arms dejectedly down to her sides; her right elbow hit her satchel. Instantly she was reminded that the book of 'EL' was right here in her satchel, and it had been with her the whole time. Surely this special book everyone was after had *some kind* of directions in it to help her figure a way out of this mess! She quickly pulled the book out of her satchel and laid it gently on the floor beside her. She skimmed through the pages…and stopped on the page marked

"FREEZING TIME SPELL"

She read it out loud:

COME TO ME O' GODDESS OF TIME,

BY SECOND, BY MINUTE, BY HOUR, BY DAY,

MAKE TIME BE MINE,

THIS TO YOU I SAY!


When the last word left her lips, she looked up from the book… and all of the Mortar soldiers were standing there…frozen in time. She rushed to Poseidon's side only to find, that *he* was frozen as well! Tears started running down her face, and just as Demetra began to wrap her arms around him, she noticed that Cree was standing beside her with King Poseidon's Trident in his hand. "Stand back Demetra!" Cree exclaimed as he placed Poseidon's Trident in his hand and with a blinding white hot flash, King Poseidon was no longer frozen. As Poseidon looked around he could not believe that his kingdom had been reduced to such rubble. "I never dreamed this would or could happen," Poseidon said dejectedly. "King Poseidon, sir," Demetra said gently, "We have to get you some place safe and quickly." Poseidon nodded his head and sadly followed Cree and Demetra back to the Crystal Healing Cavern where Turr was resting and hopefully recuperating. When they arrived back at the Healing Cavern, Demetra found a good as new Turr and Charlie's leg was healed as well. Charlie said "Demetra, are you alright?" She replied "Yes, but I am afraid Atlantis is not. We have brought King Poseidon with us so he can recuperate." The friends gathered together in front of Poseidon. "King Poseidon, we must find your daughter, Amalta. She is just one of the four that we will need in order to end this madness. Please help us!" Demetra begged. "I always hoped that this day would never come, but yet here it is, right before me. There is only one thing left to do," Poseidon said regally. Suddenly, he grabbed his trident and rammed it clear through is chest, piercing his heart. A single drop of metallic silver blood dropped to the cavern floor. As the blood hit the floor his body quickly reduced into a pool of beautiful turquoise blue seawater. His golden trident stood pointing straight up from the cavern floor, with no help at all. A shimmering silver light lingered around it, flowing like a waterfall that had no source. Abruptly the light was absorbed by the trident. The Trident flew up in the air and headed straight for Demetra's head. It was as if someone had thrown a spear at her. She leaned out of the way, stuck her arm out and snatched it from midair. Eyes wide in amazement, she grasped it firmly in her fist as booming thunder sounded and a brilliant flash of white hot lightning made her eyes close. She opened her eyes to find…………..

# Chapter 11
# The Bermuda Triangle

A beautiful shoreline?

She was standing on a beautiful shoreline! With her friends beside her! The Trident was in her hand. She could feel a warm, balmy breeze on her face and she knew that she was no longer in Atlantis. As she turned her gaze from the beach all she could see on both sides and behind her was thick jungle. "What should we do now Turr?" Demetra asked. "I'm not so sure Demetra. One things for sure I don't think we are here by accident, the Trident brought us here for a reason. Amalta has to be here somewhere." As the friend's looked around Charlie was quick to point out a trail not too far in the distance. "Let's start there," Charlie insisted and they all walked toward the trail. The friends traveled down the path for what seemed like forever, before finally approaching what appeared to be a small village. Although it was eerily quiet Demetra decided to shout out a "HELLO!" The friends walked around and came to the conclusion that the village seemed empty. They were soon proved wrong. Out of nowhere they were suddenly surrounded by a group of village people pointing spears and sharp objects at their faces. The villagers shouted at them in their strange native tongue. It was a language that none of the friend knew anything about. Just then a loud, strong voice shouted over the noise of the crowd **Stop**! **Silence**! Stepping out from the crowd was a beautiful young girl with long flowing blond hair. The sunlight glistened off her hair like it was spun gold. She walked straight up to Demetra, peered into her eyes and reached for the Trident. "I know who you are and I know why you are here." The girl said as she pulled down the neck of her tattered tan shirt to reveal three bloody puncture wounds. "I felt everything." The girl said sadly as a tear ran from her eye and down her cheek. "Amalta?" Demetra asked. "Yes, I am

Amalta Poseidon. When my father took his life I received his pain *and* saw his very last vision. His last vision was of you Demetra Scott." Demetra handed the Trident to her and said "THIS obviously belongs to you." "Come." Amalta said regally. "We must dine." Over a dinner of roasted pork and fresh mangos, Demetra could not help but wonder where they were. "The Bermuda Triangle," Amalta said. Demetra looked at her, eyes wide in disbelief. "I can read minds Demetra Scott. That is a power I have been blessed with since I was born. I was placed here at birth by my father. This beautiful island is hidden from the outside world. It has never been reached by anyone, other than my father and the other Elemental Kings and Queen, my aunt, and uncles. The book of 'EL', that is now in your possession, is the only way an outsider can find us. I suggest that you keep it safe, at all cost. As you already know, the Elemental King and Queens can't be killed by anyone or anything. They have to purposely take their own lives with their last thought being of their children when they do so. That way no one can make them end their own lives if it is not entirely of their own free will. Now that my father has given his life for your quest, I suggest we find the other Elementals...but my question to you, Demetra Scott, is what do we do now?" Turr looked at them and said "We have to push forward and go to the next elemental realm. The sooner, the better, I am afraid. Tagu will not stop until he gets what he is after. Now I'm afraid he knows that we are trying to stop him." Suddenly a brisk wind blew through the fire they were sitting around causing glowing red hot embers to fly high into the air. The book that was sitting by Demetra's side flew open, the pages fluttered in the wind finally stopping to reveal a page labeled simply **AIR**. The friends studied the page. Positioned right in the middle of the page was a map labeled Shangri-La. "Turr, what do you think? Can you get us there?" Asked Charlie "Yes." answered Turr "It will be no problem. I think we should finish eating, get some sleep and head out at first light."

# Chapter 12
# Thieves in the night

As the friends slept peacefully in their huts nestled high in the trees. A large sweaty hand clamped over Demetra's mouth, snatching her from her bed. Shaken and scared she realized that she was being dragged outside and down the tree. Looking over her shoulder she realized that Charlie, Turr, Cree and Amalta had all met with the same fate. Captured by Mortars! "The book! Get the book!" Demetra screamed as she watched the book being carried away by the same evil face that she had looked upon in Atlantis…and in her dream. Their captors gathered them up and carried them to a huge steel basket. Once they were inside their captors slammed and locked the door of the basket. Demetra shouted "LET US GO!" The ghastly leader thrust his face up to the bars of the cage and with spittle flying from his mouth his deep voice bellowed "No! Your gods have run things long enough! It is time that the rightful ruler reigns." A Mortar solider yelled from the distance "Malik, the Wrens are ready!" Malik, Demetra thought, she had heard that name before. Tilly the leaf sprite told her who Malik was. She said he was the leader of the Mortar army, now Demetra understood it all. The creature she had battled with, in her dream, was Malik the leader of the Mortar Army! She felt in Atlantis that he was the leader of the pack, know his name confirmed it. As he walked away Demetra watched the book walk away with him. "All is lost," Demetra said sadly. "What are we going to do?" Turr touched her shoulder and said gently "It's going to be okay. We *will* find a way out of this mess." "Mount up!" Malik said to his Mortar soldiers, and they all jumped onto the back of the Wrens. As they took off one of the Wrens grabbed the steel basket with its sharp claws and off they flew into the night. As the friends stood helpless, their faces pressed to the bars of their cage Demetra asked "What are we going to do? We *have* to get to Shangri-La, and find the Air King before Tagu, and that nasty Malik do, or all will be lost." "Don't worry," Amalta said, "we will get out of this." "Where are they taking us?" Demetra asked softly. The friends decided to huddle together and as they flew through the dark midnight sky Demetra sat there, mesmerized by the bright, twinkling stars. "Beautiful aren't they." Amalta said "Did you know that every star is the soul of a person? When a human dies their soul is changed into a star, that way the dead can always look down from the heavens and guide their loved ones." "I wonder if my mother is up there." Charlie said sadly. Amalta placed her hand on Charlie's shoulder and said softly "I'm sure she's there Charlie, she will always be with you." *A loud, ear piercing screech rang in their ears.* As their basket was pushed through the dark clouds, Demetra looked ahead to see a chain of dark snowcapped mountains with flames escaping from their crevices. In the distance she could see a large opening at the top of an ice capped mountain. That was their destination….and they had arrived.

# Chapter 13
# Tagu

Snatched abruptly from the basket, they were lead through winding, dark damp tunnels. The only light they had was from the flickering torches that the Mortar soldiers were carrying. They soon entered a huge room that had been carved out from inside the mountain. There, standing in the center of the stone floor was Mr. Kirk! "How could you Mr. Kirk!" Demetra shouted. "It's Tagu to you, you insufferable girl. I have had just about enough of your interference! YOU have been *nothing* but a thorn in my side." he snarled. As he turned around Demetra noticed a thick gold necklace clasped around his neck. It had a round glass charm attached. The charm was filled with a shimmering green liquid that sloshed around as he moved. "You two thought that you had outwitted me, didn't you. Sneaking into my house and stealing the book! What did you think; that you were just going to get away with it?" he snarled. "You are our teacher, Mr. Kirk! We are supposed to be able to trust you! What about the field trip to Stonehenge or is that just another part of your plan?" Demetra asked. "I told you my name is *Tagu*! When you speak to me you *will* refer to me as TAGU! I thought you were just a worthless little worm Demetra, but look, you brought me Amalta Poseidon. It appears that you have been useful after all. That is just one child less that I have to worry about capturing. Soon, I will have all of the Descendants in my grasp and Cronus will be unleashed to rule the world! Ahhh yes, Charlie and Demetra! All this time I was teaching you, watching your every move…did you think I was doing it because I wanted to? NO! I know you Charlie O'Connor and I-know-your-mother!" "What?" Charlie asked "What does my mother have to do with any of this?" Tagu lifted his staff high in the air and as a bolt of white light burst from its tip Charlie could see a cave over his shoulder light up, making the stone become translucent. There he saw his mother standing helplessly inside. "Mother!" Charlie shouted as tears flowed from his eyes. "What is the meaning of this? My mother is supposed to be dead! Why do you have her?" "Your mother didn't really die Charlie, she left you!" Tagu said hatefully. "Your mother is Gaia, Queen of the Earth Element. She left you to *try* to save her beloved Earth, but instead she fell into my trap and I imprisoned her!" "You will not get away with this!" Demetra shouted. "Ahhh…but it seems that I already have!" Tagu snatched Charlie, and Amalta's arms then yelled to the Mortar soldiers "Take the rest of them away. We leave for Shangri-La at dawn!" As the Mortar soldiers closed in on Demetra she ran to Charlie dragging her chains and yelled "**NO!** Where Charlie goes I go!" Demetra shouted. "It's okay Demetra" Charlie assured her. I will be fine. He needs me in order to free Cronus; but I will not allow that to happen! *After all I am a Gaia's son!* I *will* find a way to foil his plan to release my grandfather! Demetras eyes widened with shock as she was pulled away from Charlie, and forced to join the others. Demetra, Turr and Cree, formed a line and were led up the stone staircase and through the passageways to the cavern cells. As they neared the cells Demetra began to see Charlie's mother. The solider opened the cell door, released them of their chains, pushed them all in together, and slammed the cell door behind them. Standing there in a green tattered medieval dress with a gold bodice laced in the front. Demetra hesitantly walked toward Mrs. O' Connor, "What is going on?" Demetra asked. Gaia flipped her long brown curly hair out of the way and wrapped her arms around Demetra's neck embracing her tightly, and softly said to her, "I am so sorry, child." Gaia pulled away from Demetra and looked at her with her green eyes and gently said "I know all of this sounds so crazy to you, but if Charlie and you had known who I really was, everyone he and I love would have been in great danger. I knew when the time was right that everything would work out for the best. We Elemental Gods feared that one day Cronus would return and plague us all with his presence and wicked ways. We Elementals left our children in human hands to keep them safe. It was the only way that we could be sure that they would all be safe from Cronus' reach. "So you didn't drown in the flood?" Demetra asked. "No dear" Gaia explained. "Upon hearing rumors of the possibility of Cronus' return I conjured up the flood so that I could escape back to Eden. But alas, I was too late. Tagu was there waiting for me, and as I was about to go through the entrance into Eden, he attacked and captured me. I have been imprisoned since. I have been here waiting, wondering and worrying about what was going on, what was happening to my son. Please understand Demetra, it had to be this way." "So it's true then?" Demetra asked. "Is what true," Gaia replied. "Charlie is your son; and you must die…again! It was so hard on him when he thought you had died the first time. Now, he will have to go through it all again, he will lose you all over again, but this time it will be horrible. He will have a vision of your death just like Amalta had. She saw King Poseidon die. Charlie must suffer again, all because he **must** take your place." Gaia sadly replied to Demetra, "Unfortunately it is true. Each rightful heir must take their parents place in order to stop Cronus. When the time comes I will have to leave again, but it is the price that we must pay in order for the world to remain a safe haven for ALL its inhabitants. Turr interrupted their reunion by asking how they were going to get out of here. "The whole place is surrounded by Mortar's what can we do?" Cree stepped in with a big smile, taking over the conversation by saying, "Turr you *are* a shape shifter aren't you?" "Yes," Turr replied. "Well then, I, have a plan!"

# Chapter 14
# The Great Escape

"Turr this is what we are going to do. First, you need to turn yourself into Malik," Cree explained. "Then as the leader of his army you can pass by unnoticed and then … go fetch the book!" "Alone?" he asked. "Yes you can do it!" "Ok…Then how are we going to get out of this cell and better yet, how will we a get off this mountain? It is littered with Mortars and Wrens!" "Disguised as Malik you can easily sneak past the guards and find the book. If you run into trouble…well, I'm sure you will think of something." Cree said with a grin. "Okay here goes nothing." Turr said nervously. He transformed himself into a tiny red lizard glistening with black speckles, and crawled through the iron grates of the cell. "Uck! Couldn't you have picked something small and furry over some nasty little lizard" Demetra exclaimed. Once outside the cell he crawled into a nearby crevice, where his lizard form transformed into an identical match of Malik. He gave the friends a wink and told them to sit tight. Turr walked right past the soldiers as they stuffed their faces with food like pigs! Disgusting Turr thought as he went down the same stairway they were led up earlier. He entered the stone room where they had originally met Tagu, only to find that the room was empty! There was nothing there, the room was totally empty! Suddenly a voice shouted from down one of the passageways "**Hurry up**!" Turr immediately recognized it as being Tagu's voice. He tiptoed quietly toward the voice peering into rooms on the left and right as he passed them. He quickly found the book in one of the rooms. It was lying on a table, surrounded by candlelight. Thankfully, no one was in the room with it! It could not be *that* easy Turr thought. He stood there for a moment, waiting to see if Tagu or the real Malik showed up. After realizing that the coast was clear, Turr walked right inside the room very quickly and snatched the book off the table. He placed it under his arm, turned around and headed for the doorway. On his way out he noticed Amalta's Trident in the same room as well. It was right there leaning in the corner! They obviously didn't allow her to take it when they took her away with Charlie. He quickly grabbed it and walked out of the room. Unnoticed he walked down the passageway and back up the stairs. As he rounded a corner, near their cell, Turr found himself face to face with the real Malik! The real Malik let out a loud, bellowing yell signaling the entire Mortar army that there was trouble! Turr could not help feeling very frightened. "What I am going to do now?" He thought, *Dragon!* That's what I'll do. So, *as the real Malik reached for the book Turr jerked it away from him and transformed himself into a massive blood red dragon with large black scales scattered around his body.* Turrs large smoke gray wings overshadowed Malik's hulking frame. Turr turned and slung Malik violently into the wall of the mountain with his long rough, scaly tail. He rushed to the cell to gather his friends. "Stand back!" Turr shouted. He sunk his dragon talons into the cold steel gate and ripped it from its hinges...just like it was nothing at all, freeing his friends! "Hurry, jump on!" Turr knelt down and stuck his scaly leg out, allowing them all easy access onto his back. As Demetra climbed on she said with a big smile, "Turr I have to say I like this lizard a whole lot better!" With a wink he nudged her onto his back and made sure everyone was aboard. He flew through the passageways, swerving left and right. Approaching them from the cave entrance was what looked like the *entire* army of Mortars! WHOOOSH! *Turr released hot blue flames from his dragon mouth, cooking the Mortar soldiers like they were fried chicken! He continued flying quickly thru the entrance, and with a swish of his big scaly tail, Turr made his spectacular exit!* As they flew through the air Gaia sensed that something was troubling Demetra. "Don't worry child, Charlie will be okay," Gaia assured Demetra. "I hope so, Mrs. O'Connor, I really do hope so!"

# Chapter 15
# An Evil Plot

"How could you let this happen?" Tagu shouted angrily at Malik. "I'm sorry sir I was no match for a dragon," he mumbled. "This throws everything off." Tagu began to throw things around the room. "What am I supposed to do now?" he yelled. Malik said "I will assemble the army; we will be after them in no time!" "NO!" Tagu shouted "This is what we will do. I have the Earth and Water Descendants; let's allow the others to do the work for us. We will allow them to get to Shangri-La and once they find the 'Air' and 'Fire' Descendants we will take action. The other Elementals will give up their children's location to Gaia, the shape shifter, fish boy and that nuisance Demetra. It will be like taking candy from a baby." Tagu held his orb necklace tightly and said "Then, when we have all of the Descendants in one place, we can finally release Cronus. Get a few of your soldiers ready Malik, you will need to follow them to Shangri-La, unnoticed." "Yes sir, right away." As Malik left the room Tagu walked over to his shiny silver bowl. Once there he began to stare deeply into the bowl of liquid, with a touch of his finger he sent ripples in the liquid. The ripples revealed Turr flying through the air with his friends on his back. As Tagu watched them flying through the night sky he grasped his necklace and said, "Soon my Lord you will be unleashed and together we will rule the world!" Charlie shouted from the corner were Malik had chained him to the wall "I am son of Gaia! You will never get away with this Tagu, Mr. Kirk or whatever you want to call yourself. We will stop you!" "I'm counting on it Charlie O'Connor! I am counting on it!" Tagu exclaimed.

# Chapter 16
# Shangri-La

Demetra began to feel the warm humid air hitting her face. "We must be getting close," she said to her friends. As they flew around the mountains, the horizon was spectacular with the tan, peach and orange colors of the rising sun. As the light revealed Shangri-La to them, they were amazed to see such a beautiful landscape. It was filled with lush dark green grass, flowering trees and crystal clear pools of water. Different color flowers bloomed profusely throughout the grass and filled the air with a wonderful sweet fragrance. Positioned in the center of the valley was an extraordinary temple made of precious stones that glimmered in the morning light. Turr landed at the foot of the main stairway and they were quickly greeted by a group of monks, dressed in dark brown robes. As they climbed down off Turr's scaly back, he transformed himself back into his human form. "Are you alright?" Demetra asked Turr. "Yes," he said, "just a little tired is all." "I know Turr we are all pretty darn tired, hopefully we will rest soon." They followed the monks up the stairs and into the main entrance of the temple. They were led down a long hall, which opened up into a great room. As they walked through the huge wooden doors the Air God and his Queen stood up from their thrones and began to walk toward them. Gaia walked up and said, "I'm sorry Brother, but the time has come. We must summon your son. Ilmater must take his place at the ancient stone table, for that is the only chance we have to stop Cronus and Tagu." "Agreed," the Air God replied. "Forgive me," Gaia exclaimed "this is Queen Eos and King Aeolus. King Aeolus is my brother and he is the God of Air." In despair King Aeolus acknowledged that he knew what he had to do. King Aeolus summoned one of the nearby monks to come forth. "It is time," he said softly. With a gentle nod the monk walked away. "All of you must stand here in this very spot for when I pass, this circle will transport you directly to my son, Ilmater." King Aeolus turned to face his wife; he gently took her hands in his and pulled her close. He calmly kissed her lips and wiped a tear from her eye. "Take care of our son, my love." "I will," she said quietly. Queen Eos rubbed her husband's face with both her soft white hands as tears ran silently down her cheeks. The couple walked to a nearby table where they could have a few precious moments' alone. The monk King Aeolus had summoned earlier returned with a golden goblet, filled with liquid. He carried it carefully between both hands. Being careful not to spill it, with sadness in his eyes, he handed it to King Aeolus. The King placed the goblet to his lips and drank deeply. It was the last drink he would ever have. As the golden goblet hit the floor his soul began to whisk through the air like flower petals dancing in the wind. Suddenly, a violent tornado erupted and whisked the group of friends away

# Chapter 17
# Poison

As the tornado winds calmed down they found themselves high on a grassy cliff overlooking the ocean. They watched the waves crashing on the rocks far below them. "Where are we?" Cree asked. "I'm not sure," Demetra said "but Ilmater cannot be far." Demetra touched her satchel just to reassure herself that the book was still there. "It's there." Turr said to Demetra. "Let's go children," Gaia said. They walked away from the cliff's edge and rounded a huge boulder to find a small quaint village. In the distance, grazing in lush emerald pastures were hundreds of goats and dairy cows. The village was made up of around twenty homes. They were made of stone with thatch roofs. The group of friends entered the village to find everyone staring at them. Whispers began to fill the air from the villagers. Just ahead, standing at a well, was a man wearing a rough brown cloak. He turned and looked at them. "Arr ye lost?" the man asked with a Scottish accent. "I'm sorry to bother you sir but we have traveled so far, could we trouble you for some sleeping quarters and some food for the night?" "Aye," the man said. "Me name be Duff and I am surra we could find some way to help ya for the night." The man led them to a stable. "Here ya arr ya can sleep here fer the night it's all that I have. I'll be having me wife bring ya some food once yew arr settled." "We are ever so grateful sir," Gaia said. "I will leave ya to it then," Duff said. "Thank you," they all replied, and with that Duff closed the stable doors. "Pew it smells like poop in here!" Cree said. "Yes it does, but it is all we have so let's just deal with it for tonight, Okay?" replied Gaia. As they all began to get comfortable a heart wrenching scream came from the direction of Duffs home. They quickly ran across the yard toward the home to see what was wrong. When they reached the front door, they were met by Duff walking out of his home in distress, tears running down his kind face. Demetra's eyes were widened with fear as she pushed through the doorway only to find Duffs wife, sitting on the floor, sobbing mournfully, holding the lifeless body of their son. Gaia pushed Demetra aside to reveal a cup that was on the floor beside the boys' lifeless body. Gaia put the cup to her nose "Poison!" she exclaimed. From the doorway Turr yelled **"Stop!"** They all jumped up to see who Turr was yelling at. **"Stop him!"** Demetra exclaimed. Turr ran the mysterious man down and jumped on his back pushing him to the ground. He grabbed the man turning him over, to reveal the same monk from Shangri-La. The very same monk King Aeolus summoned to bring him the poison.

Made in the USA
Las Vegas, NV
07 June 2024

90840491R00046